For Ruby and Ivy, who love to swim.
With love,

T.H.N.

❥

For my daughter, Ivy Kathleen McFadden

D.E.

Sleeping Bear Press
2395 South Huron Parkway, Suite 200
Ann Arbor, MI 48104
www.sleepingbearpress.com

Printed and bound in the United States.

10 9 8 7 6 5 4 3 2 1

Library of Congress Cataloging-in-Publication Data

Names: Noble, Trinka Hakes, author. | Ettlinger, Doris, illustrator.
Title: The legend of sea glass / written by Trinka Hakes Noble ; illustrated
by Doris Ettlinger.
Description: Ann Arbor, MI : Sleeping Bear Press, [2016] | Summary: "An
original legend explaining the origin of sea glass, those small pieces of
colored glass found and collected on beaches. This tale attributes it to the
tears of mermaids, weeping for lives lost at sea"—Provided by publisher.
Identifiers: LCCN 2015027638 | ISBN 9781585366118
Subjects: | CYAC: Mermaids—Fiction. | Sea glass—Fiction.
Classification: LCC PZ7.N6715 Lek 2016 | DDC [Fic]—dc23
LC record available at http://lccn.loc.gov/2015027638

The Legend *of* Sea Glass

By Trinka Hakes Noble ✳ *Illustrated by* Doris Ettlinger

$\mathcal{L}$ong ago there was a time when men did not sail the seven seas. Nor did explorers navigate the wide deep oceans in tall ships, searching for distant lands. Even fishermen stayed in the shallow water, close to shore.

No one ventured out beyond the sight of land for in those days it was believed that the world was flat. No one dared sail past the horizon, for if they did, they would surely fall off the edge of the earth where savage sea monsters were waiting to devour them!

So people lived safely on land.

Yet, they were drawn to the ocean, gazing out in wonder at its endless, blue expanse. People who lived along the shoreline and beaches collected beautiful shells and stones, turning them into adornments and treasured keepsakes. They traded the stones and seashells with inland people for they were of great value and beauty.

But far beyond their view, and even further beyond their wildest imaginations, there lived a world of mysterious sea creatures that were half girl and half fish. These maidens of the sea had splendid flowing tails and long graceful hair that swayed like seaweed in the ocean's currents. By nature they were shy, gentle creatures. They were called mermaids.

The mighty ocean loved the mermaids for they were the most magnificent creatures in its entire domain. It favored the mermaids with its warm salty waters that never froze. It nourished them with its bounty. It sheltered the mermaids with its deep calm waters, protecting them from storms and rough seas.

Below, on the ocean floor, the mermaids built little playhouses for their underwater friends. They also tended gardens of bright corral and groves of tall seaweed.

The mermaids loved living in the ocean, playing water tag with the dolphins and other sea creatures.

Seals and sea otters frolicked among the tall seaweed, playing hide-and-seek with the mermaids, while schools of radiant fish swam in their corral-reef gardens.

On sunny days the shy mermaids would come to the surface and lie on the warm rocks near the shoreline, making sure they were hidden from view. There they would bask in the sunshine as they preened their magnificent tails.

And for a great long time the mermaids were very happy, which deeply pleased the ocean.

But one day while the mermaids were sunning themselves, a soft sea breeze suddenly turned into a stiff offshore wind. Waves swelled and crashed against their rocks. The mermaids were just about to return to the calm ocean floor when something caught their eye. Peeking from behind their rocks, they saw a fisherman's boat bobbing wildly in the waves. It came closer and closer, careening toward their rocks.

Suddenly there was a loud crash of splintering wood, then a cry for help. Without hesitation, the mermaids dove into the rough waters and pulled a small boy from the swirling sea.

The fisherman stared in amazement as the mermaids gently placed his young son on the rocks, then quickly swam out of sight.

"Oh, thank you, thank you!" the fisherman called after them.

When the fisherman and his son safely returned to land, they told everyone what had happened.

"Such beautiful sea creatures, half girl and half fish!" the man exclaimed.

The other fishermen listened intently for this was the first time anyone had actually seen these creatures. "I tell you, they saved my boy!"

As time passed, more and more stories were told of mermaids saving fishermen at sea. Eventually, people learned the world was not flat and there was no danger of falling off the edge. So more and more ships sailed the seas.

The ships grew bigger and carried many passengers. Now, when there was a storm at sea or a shipwreck, more and more people needed rescuing. The mermaids saved as many as they could.

One day the sky turned an angry black as a large group of
ships was crossing the ocean. Gale-force winds whipped the
waves into a deadly frenzy. The powerful waves and lashing
winds damaged many of the ships, some breaking in half.
Many people needed rescuing. The mermaids quickly rushed
toward the surface. Even the smallest wanted to help, and she
swam after them as fast as she could.

"No, no!" said one of her older sister mermaids.
"You are too small. You must stay behind."
But the little mermaid had a brave heart
and secretly followed them.

When the little mermaid got to the surface, she saw a young sailor caught in a wave, which was carrying him far from his ship. She swam after him with all her might, but a gigantic wave caught her and tossed her back. When she came up again, the sailor was nowhere to be seen. Darting here and there, she searched and searched, but couldn't find him.

"I won't forget you," she cried.

When the storm had passed, the sad little mermaid was alone on a rock, her young heart nearly broken. And, for the first time ever, a mermaid shed a tear. A sad tear for the young sailor she could not save. This tiny tear slipped into the ocean.

"What's this I feel? A mermaid's tear?" asked the mighty ocean. "This cannot be!"

So the mighty ocean saved that first tiny tear, and the many mermaid tears that followed for all those lost at sea. With its strong salty surf, endless waves, and countless tides, the ocean changed the mermaids' tears into beautiful glass gems.

"These gems shall be all the colors of the mermaids' tails," it declared. "That way their tears shall never be lost in my vast waters but will last forever."

The glass gems began a long journey.